D1461282

For David

William Collins Sons & Co Ltd
London · Glasgow · Sydney · Auckland
Toronto · Johannesburg

First published 1980
Fourteenth impression 1984

ISBN 0 00 183922 5
Origination by Culver Graphics Litho Ltd
Printed in Italy
by Sagdos for Imago Publishing Ltd

SPRING STORY

Jill Barklem

COLLINS

It was the most beautiful morning. The spring sunshine crept into every cottage along Brambly Hedge, and the little windows in the trees were opened wide.

All the mice were up early, but earliest of all was Wilfred, who lived with his family in the hornbeam tree. It was Wilfred's birthday.

Jumping out of bed, he ran into his parents' room, and bounced on their bed till they gave him their presents.

"Happy birthday, Wilfred," said Mr. and Mrs. Toadflax sleepily.

He tore off the pretty wrappings, and scattered them all over the floor. His squeaks of excitement woke his brother and sisters.

His parents turned over to go to sleep again. Wilfred went and sat on the stairs and blew his new whistle.

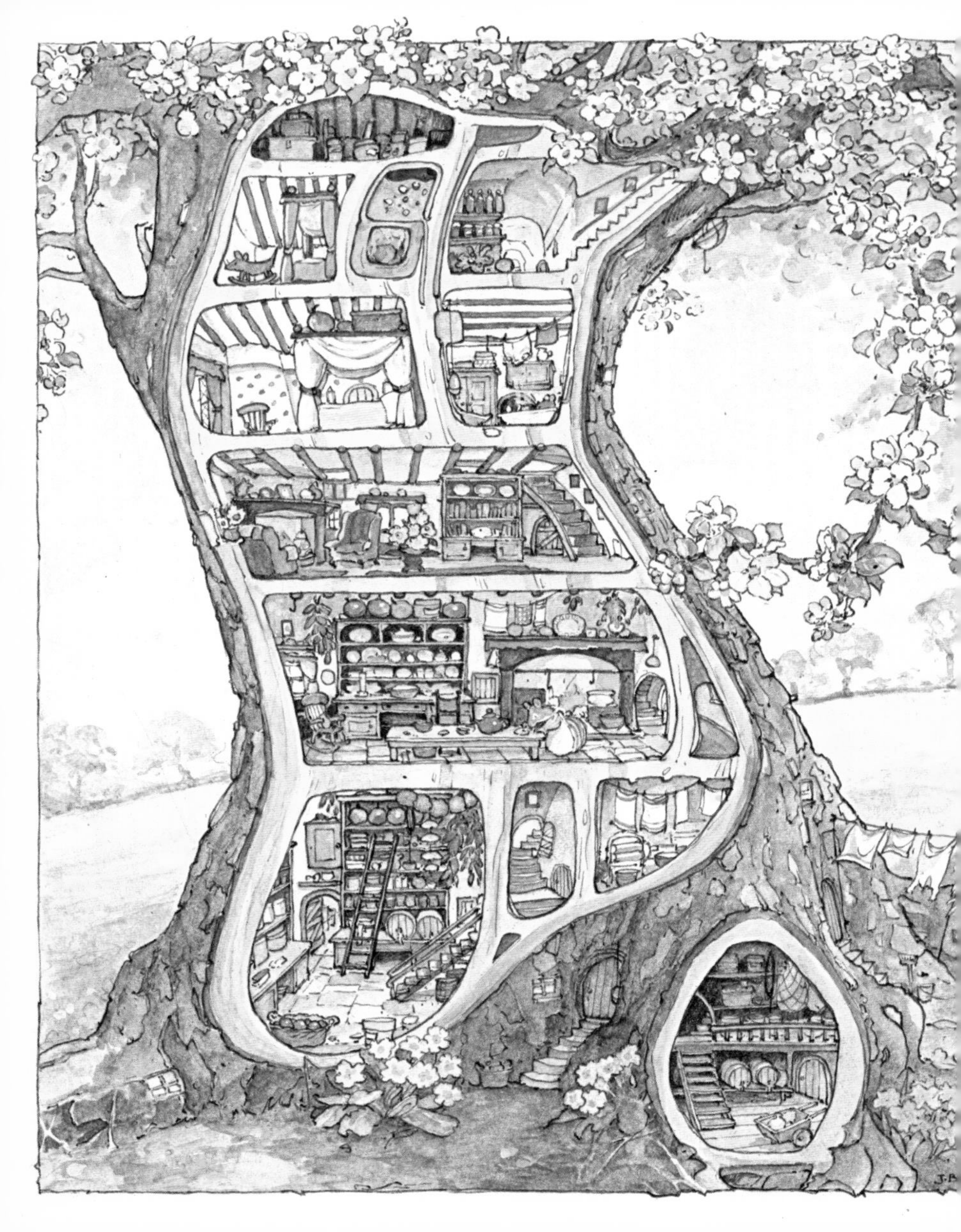

Mr. and Mrs. Apple lived next door at Crabapple Cottage. The sound of Wilfred's whistle floated in through their bedroom window Mrs. Apple got up and stretched. She sniffed the sweet air and went down to the kitchen to make a pot of elderflower tea. She was a very kindly mouse and a wonderful cook. The cottage always smelled of newly-made bread, fresh cakes and blackberry puddings.

"Breakfast's ready," she called. Mr. Apple got out of bed with a sigh, and joined her at the kitchen table. They ate their toast and jam, and listened to Wilfred's warbling.

"I think somebody needs a lesson from the blackbird," said Mr. Apple, brushing the crumbs from his whiskers and putting on his coat.

Mr. Apple was a nice, old-fashioned sort of mouse. He was warden of the Store Stump where all the food for Brambly Hedge was kept.

The Store Stump was not far away. As Mr. Apple walked happily through the grass to the big front doors, he felt someone pull his tail. He turned around quickly. It was Wilfred, whistle in hand.

"It's my birthday!" he squeaked.

"Is it, young mouse," said Mr. Apple. "Happy birthday to you! Would you like to come and help me check the Store Stump? We'll see what we can find."

In the middle of the Stump was an enormous hall, and leading off from it many passages and staircases. These led in turn to dozens of storerooms full of nuts and honey and jams and pickles. Each one had to be inspected. Wilfred's legs felt tired by the time they had finished, and he sat by the fire in the hall to rest. Mr. Apple lifted down a jar of sugared violets. He made a little cornet from a twist of paper, and filled it with sweets. Taking Wilfred by the paw, he led him through the dark corridors out into the sun. Wilfred went to look for his brother, and Mr. Apple hurried down the hedge to visit his daughter Daisy and her husband, Lord Woodmouse.

J.B

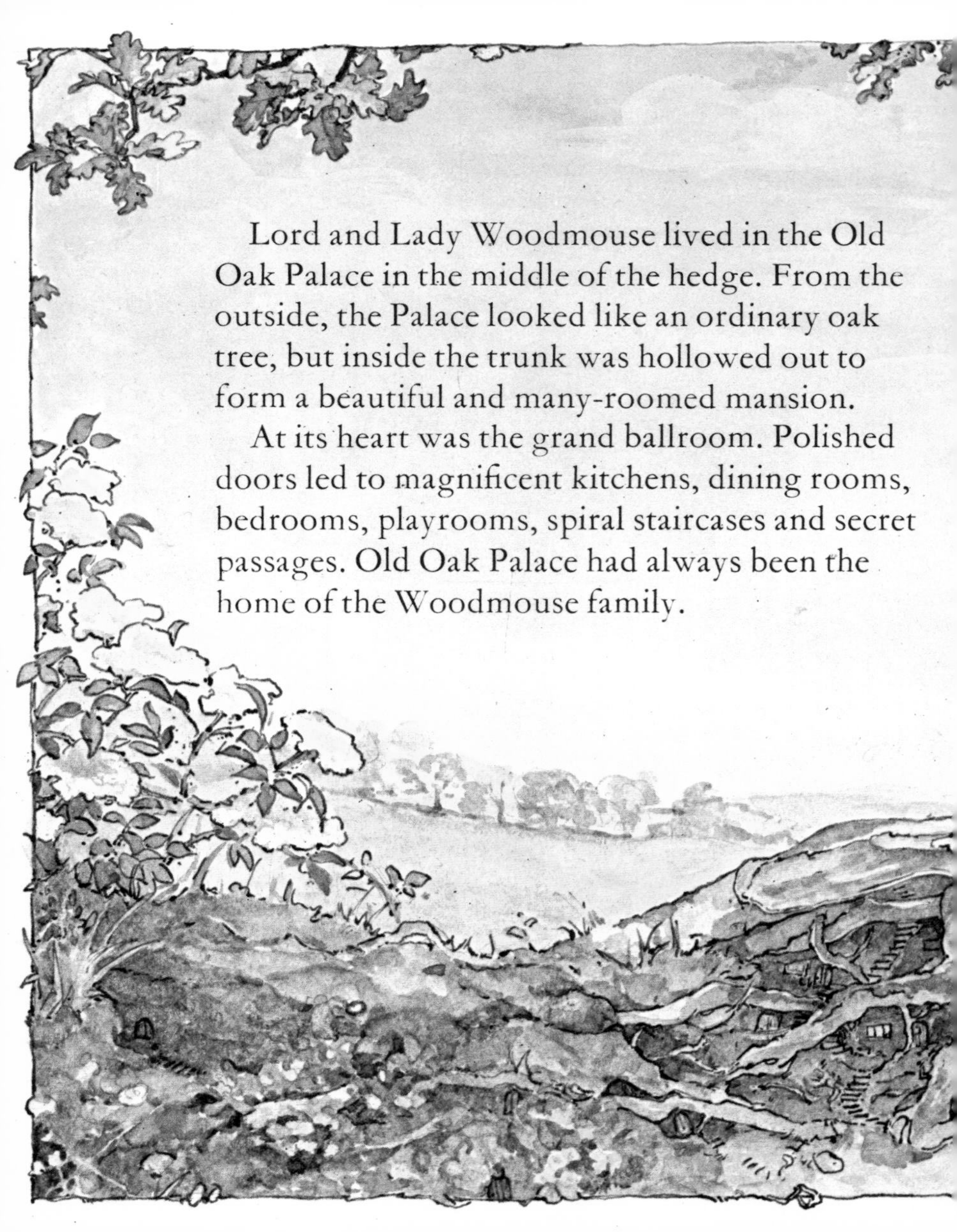

Lord and Lady Woodmouse lived in the Old Oak Palace in the middle of the hedge. From the outside, the Palace looked like an ordinary oak tree, but inside the trunk was hollowed out to form a beautiful and many-roomed mansion.

At its heart was the grand ballroom. Polished doors led to magnificent kitchens, dining rooms, bedrooms, playrooms, spiral staircases and secret passages. Old Oak Palace had always been the home of the Woodmouse family.

Upstairs in the best bedroom, Lord and Lady Woodmouse woke to bright sunshine.

"What a perfect day!" sighed Lady Daisy as she nibbled a primrose biscuit. When they heard that Daisy's father had come to call, they were soon up and dressed and running down the winding stairs to greet him.

They found him in the kitchen drinking mint tea with Mrs. Crustybread, the Palace cook. Daisy gave Mr. Apple a kiss and sat down beside him.

"Hello Papa," she said. "What brings you here so early?"

"I've just met little Wilfred – it's his birthday today. Shall we arrange a surprise picnic for him?"

"What a wonderful idea," said Lord Woodmouse. Daisy nodded.

"I'll make him a special birthday cake if his mother agrees," said Mrs. Crustybread, hurrying off to the pantry to find the ingredients.

Everyone was to be invited of course, so Mr. Apple set off up the hedge towards the woods, and Lord Woodmouse went down towards the stream calling at each house on the way.

The first house on Mr. Apple's route was Elderberry Lodge. This fine elder bush was Basil's home. Basil was in charge of the Store Stump cellars. He was just getting up.

"A picnic eh? Splendid! I'll bring up some rose petal wine," he said, shuffling absent-mindedly round the room looking for his trousers. Basil had long white whiskers and always wore a scarlet waistcoat. He used to keep the other mice amused for hours with his stories.

"Ah, there you are, you rascals," he exclaimed, discovering his trousers behind the sofa.

Next Mr. Apple came to the hornbeam. Mr. Toadflax was sitting on his front doorstep eating bread and bramble jelly.

"We thought it would be nice to have a surprise picnic for your Wilfred," whispered Mr. Apple. "We won't tell him what it's for, and we'll all meet at midday by the Palace roots."

Mr. Toadflax was delighted with the suggestion, and went inside to tell his wife. Mr. Apple went on to visit Old Vole who lived in a tussock of grass in the middle of the field.

Lord Woodmouse, meanwhile, was working his way down to the stream. The news had travelled ahead of him, and all along the hedge excited mice leaned out of their windows to ask when the picnic would take place.

"I'll see if I can find some preserves," said old Mrs. Eyebright.

"Shall we bring tablecloths?" called the weavers who lived in the tangly hawthorn trees.

Poppy Eyebright from the dairy promised cheeses, and Dusty Dogwood, the Miller, offered a batch of buns.

Mice soon began calling at the Store Stump to collect clover flour and honey, bramble brandy and poppy seeds, and all the other good things needed for the picnic. Mrs. Crustybread baked a huge hazelnut cake with layers of thick cream, and Wilfred's mother decorated it. Mrs. Apple made some of her special primrose puddings.

Wilfred knew that there was to be an outing, and that if he behaved, he would be allowed to go. He did his best but with a new whistle, a drum and a peashooter for his birthday, it wasn't easy.

When the Toadflax family arrived at the Palace, Wilfred was rather disappointed that no one there seemed to know that it was his birthday. Indeed he had rather hoped for a few more presents, but

it would have been rude to drop hints, so he hid his feelings as best he could. At a signal from Lord Woodmouse they all set off with their baskets, hampers and wheelbarrows.

Everyone had something to carry. Wilfred was given an enormous basket, so heavy he could hardly lift it. Mr. Apple lent him a wheelbarrow, and his brother and sisters helped him to push it, but still poor Wilfred found it hard to keep up.

It was a very long way. Heaving and pulling, wheeling and hauling, the mice made their way round the Palace, through the cornfield and up by the stream. Wilfred felt very hot and he wanted a rest.

“Here we are!” cried Lord Woodmouse at last.
The baskets were put down and opened, and nettlestem cloths spread out on the mossy grass. In no time at all, the food was unpacked. Wilfred was exhausted. He sat on his basket, too tired to open it, his whiskers drooping sadly.

Mr. Apple said grace: "For this good food from our green fields, may we be very grateful."

"I think the knives are in your basket, Wilfred," said Mrs. Apple kindly. "If you get them out, we can cut the pies."

Slowly, Wilfred slipped from his perch and undid the catch. When he lifted the lid, he could hardly believe his eyes.

Inside the hamper, packed all around with presents, was an enormous cake, and on the top, written in pink icing, was HAPPY BIRTHDAY WILFRED.

"*Happy Birthday, dear Wilfred,*
Happy Birthday to you," sang the mice.

When Wilfred had opened all his presents, Basil said, "Give us a tune," so he bashfully stood up and played *Hickory, Dickory, Dandelion Clock* on his new whistle. Mrs. Toadflax nudged him meaningfully when he had finished.

"Er . . . thank you for all my lovely presents," said Wilfred, trying to avoid Mrs. Crustybread's eye. She had caught him firing acorns through her kitchen window earlier in the day.

"Now for tea," announced Daisy Woodmouse.
The mice sat on the grass and Wilfred handed round the cake.

When tea was over, the grown-ups snoozed under the bluebells, while the young mice played hide-and-seek in the primroses.

At last the sun began to sink behind the Far Woods, and a chilly breeze blew over the field. It was time to go home.

When the moon came up that night, Brambly Hedge was silent and still. Every mouse was fast asleep.